George Brown, CLASS CLOWN

Eww! What's on My Shoe?

GROSSET & DUNLAP
Published by the Penguin Group
Penguin Group (USA), 375 Hudson Street, New York, New York 10014, USA

USA | Canada | UK | Ireland | Australia | New Zealand | India | South Africa | China
Penguin Books Ltd, Registered Offices: 80 Strand, London WC2R 0RL, England

For more information about the Penguin Group visit penguin.com

Text copyright © 2013 by Nancy Krulik. Illustrations copyright © 2013 by Aaron Blecha. All rights reserved. Published by Grosset & Dunlap, a division of Penguin Young Readers Group, 345 Hudson Street, New York, New York 10014. GROSSET & DUNLAP is a trademark of Penguin Group (USA). Printed in the U.S.A.

Library of Congress Cataloging-in-Publication Data is available.

ISBN 978-0-448-46114-4   10 9 8 7 6 5 4 3 2 1

George Brown, CLASS CLOWN

Eww! What's on My Shoe?

by Nancy Krulik

illustrated by Aaron Blecha

Grosset & Dunlap
An Imprint of Penguin Group (USA)

Chapter 1

"*Eww!* This one's *really* gooey!" George Brown shouted excitedly as he peeled a huge blob of pink gum from under the seat at the bus stop. "I think it was *just* chewed."

"Awesome, dude," George's best friend, Alex, said. "The fresh stuff always sticks the best." He opened a plastic bag, and George dropped the glob in with the rest of the pieces of already been chewed gum the boys had collected that morning.

"**Your ABC gum ball must be huge by now,**" George said.

"Yep. In fact, the ball's so massive, I have to keep it in a shed in the backyard."

Alex told him. "Besides, my mom doesn't want it in the house. She says having a ball made of gum that's been in other people's mouths is disgusting."

George didn't understand that at all. Alex's mom was a dentist. She had her hands in other people's mouths all day long. What was the difference?

"Isn't a gum ball that size big enough to get you into the *Schminess Book of World Records*?" George wondered aloud.

"Not really," Alex said. "But it's getting there. I measured it yesterday, and I think I only need a few more layers to **break the world record**."

"Well, today's Sunday," George said, "which means we have all day to go around town and find gum. You'll have your picture in the *Schminess Book of World Records* in no time!"

Alex pulled a glob of pink bubble gum from a tree trunk. "Amazing where people will stick their gum," he said as he popped it into his plastic bag and looked around. "I think we've gotten all the gum we're gonna get here."

"Yeah," George agreed. "So where do you think we should go next?"

Alex thought for a second. "How about Ernie's Ice Cream Emporium?" he suggested. "People have to take the gum out of their mouths to eat ice cream. And when they do, they don't have any place to put it except under the table. There are always **mounds of gum** under those tables."

"Ernie's?" George's voice cracked nervously. "I don't think I want to go there. I mean, that's where *it* all started."

Alex knew what *it* meant. *It* was **George's magical super burp**—the cause of almost everything that had ever gone wrong in George's life since he had moved to Beaver Brook.

It all started when George and his family first arrived in town. George's dad was in the army, so the family moved around a lot. By now, George understood that first days at school could be pretty rotten. But *this* first day was the most rotten.

In his old school, George had been the class clown. He was always pulling pranks and making jokes. But George had promised himself that things were going to be different at Edith B. Sugarman Elementary School. He was turning over a new leaf. No more pranks. No more whoopee cushions or spitballs shot through straws. No more bunny ears behind people's heads. No more imitating teachers when their backs were turned.

But George didn't have to be a math genius like Alex to figure out how many friends you make being the unfunny, well-behaved new kid in school. The answer was easy: zero. Nada. Zilch.

That night, George's parents took him out to Ernie's Ice Cream Emporium. While they were sitting outside and George was finishing his root beer float, a shooting star flashed across the sky. So George made a wish.

I want to make kids laugh—but not get into trouble.

Unfortunately, the star was gone before George could finish the wish. So only half came true—the first half.

A minute later, George had a funny feeling in his belly. It was like there were **hundreds of tiny bubbles bouncing around in there**. The bubbles hopped up and down and all around. They ping-ponged their way into his chest and bing-bonged their way up his throat. And then . . .

B·U·U·U·R·P!

George let out a big burp. A *huge* burp. A SUPER burp!

The super burp was loud, and it was *magic*.

Suddenly George lost control of his arms and legs. It was like they had minds of their own. His hands grabbed straws and stuck them up his nose like a walrus. His feet jumped up on the table and started dancing the hokey pokey. Everyone at Ernie's started

laughing—except George's parents, who were covered in the ice cream he'd kicked over while dancing.

The magical super burp had come back many times since then. And every time a burp came, it brought trouble with it. Like the time the super burp followed George to the fourth-grade Field Day. His burps that day were **totally out of control**. One made George bark like a dog and lick the principal's hand. Another got George into a fight with a skunk—which the skunk won. *P.U.!* That had been one bad Field Day.

Then there was the time George and his friends were putting on a backyard circus. The burp made him go crazy on his friend Chris's trampoline. George jumped so high that **his tighty whities got caught on a branch of a tree**. He wound up hanging there, in front of

everyone,
while
the tree
gave him the
world's worst
wedgie. *Ouch!*

And no
one at Edith
B. Sugarman
Elementary School
would ever forget the last art show. The
magical super burp had gone really
wacko there. George ended up squeezing
the jelly out of all the doughnuts on the
refreshment table and finger painting on
the walls. What kind of fourth-grader still
finger paints? One with a rotten super

burp, that's what kind of fourth-grader.

The super burp was always messing things up for George. And since he and the burp had first met at Ernie's, George really didn't want to go back there. Not even to help Alex.

Luckily, Alex understood. He was the only person in town who knew about the magical super burp. George hadn't actually told him about it. **He hadn't told anyone.** He knew people would think he was crazy. But Alex was smart enough to figure it out. And he was nice enough not to think George was nuts. In fact, Alex had volunteered to help George find a cure for his burp. Alex was a math and science whiz. If anyone could stop the burps, it was him.

And since his best friend was helping him out, George thought it was only fair that he help Alex out, too.

"I know an even better place to go," George told his best bud. "It's got food, fun, and lots and lots of kids. Which can only mean one thing."

Alex grinned. "Globs and globs of ABC g-u-m!"

Chapter 2

"I love **Quazy Quarters**!" George exclaimed as the boys walked into Beaver Brook's most popular arcade. "It's where I got my lava lamp. It was one hundred fifty tickets. I won almost all of them playing Skee-Ball."

"I really like your lava lamp," Alex told him. "When the gooey stuff drips inside the lamp, it reminds me of gum that's still inside someone's mouth."

"Speaking of ABC gum," George said, "here's a good-size piece." He pulled a chunk of gum from behind the door handle.

"Wow!" Alex said as George plopped

the gum into a fresh plastic bag. "You're right. This place is going to be a gold mine."

"You mean a *gum* mine," George corrected him.

Just then, George's buddy Julianna walked by. At least George *thought* it was Julianna. It was hard to tell because she was hidden behind a giant stuffed dog.

"Hey, you guys," Julianna said, putting the dog down to greet them. "Either of you want to play against me on the video car race? **Winner takes all the tickets.**"

"No thanks," George replied. "We're here on official *Schminess* business."

"Yeah," Alex said. "I'm trying to find enough ABC gum to break the record. I'm really, really close."

Julianna yanked **a piece of bright red gum** out of her mouth. "Will this help?" she asked.

Alex opened his plastic bag. "Every piece helps. Thanks."

Suddenly, George heard yelling coming from the prize booth. He turned to see his archenemy—Louie Farley—shouting at the ticket taker behind the counter.

"What do you mean you don't accept cash?" Louie yelled. "Everybody takes cash."

"Here he goes again," George said to Alex and Julianna. Louie wasn't just George's enemy. He made enemies all over town. Mostly because he was always fighting with everyone.

"Sorry, kid," the ticket taker said. "The only way you get a prize is with tickets."

"Okay, then I'll *buy* some tickets," Louie shot back. "I want enough tickets to get that giant teddy bear." He turned around and glared at Julianna. "Which is the only thing here that's bigger than your dog."

Julianna rolled her eyes.

"You can't buy tickets, either," the guy behind the counter said. "You have to *win* them."

"This is ridiculous," Louie grumbled. "Do you know how long it would take me to win enough tickets to get that bear?"

"I know!" Louie's friend Max piped up excitedly, raising his hand like he was in school. "It would take you a really long time."

"A really, *really* long time," Louie's other friend, Mike, added.

"Everything has its price," Louie continued, pulling out **a giant wad of cash**.

"Yeah," the ticket taker agreed. "And the price of this stuffed animal is two hundred fifty tickets."

Louie's face was turning really red. George thought steam might come out of his ears any second now. Which would actually be kind of cool.

"Did I mention my dad is a big, important lawyer? He's going to sue this place!" Louie shouted angrily.

"If Louie's dad sued every place Louie said he was going to, the Farleys would own all of Beaver Brook by now," George said to Alex.

George had had enough of Louie's tantrum. He had business to attend to—*sticky* business. He started to walk toward the pinball machines, but then stopped and looked down at his feet. "There's something on my shoe," he

said. He lifted his foot to discover **a huge glob of freshly chewed purple gum** on the sole of his sneaker. He peeled it off and added it to the other pieces in Alex's plastic bag.

"You guys want to go to the snack bar now?" Julianna asked.

"Okay. I think we've collected enough gum," Alex said. "Besides, I'm hungry."

"You two go ahead," George said. "I gotta stop in the bathroom first."

"While you're in there, check under the sinks," Alex suggested. "There's usually a ton of gum there."

George was definitely going to check those sinks. But before he could get anywhere near the bathroom, he felt a sinking feeling—right in the bottom of his belly. Something was bouncing around down there. Something that felt like bubbles. **Big, gassy bubbles.**

Oh no! The super burp was back.
And it wanted to play. Already it was
bing-bonging past George's bladder and
lunging toward his liver.

Uh-oh. George **shut his lips tight**—to
keep the burp from bursting out in the
middle of the arcade.

But the super burp was strong.
The bubbles ricocheted off his ribs and
trampolined on his tongue. *Bing-bong.
Ping-pong.*

George let out a burp so loud everyone
in the arcade could hear it—even over
Louie's shouting.

"Dude, no . . . ," Alex said. He hurried
over to George.

BLOOP!

Dude, *yes.* **The magical super burp was out.** George opened his mouth to say "Excuse me." But that's not what came out. Instead, his mouth shouted, "SKEE-BALL!"

George's feet leaped on top of one of the slick, shiny Skee-Ball machines. His hands picked up a ball.

"WHOAAA!" George shouted as he slipped and landed with a plop right on his rear end. His butt went sliding down the lane.

WHOOOP

iNG!

"High score!" he shouted as he dropped the ball right into the center hole.

Lights flashed. **Strips and strips of tickets flew out of the Skee-Ball machine.** George's hands didn't grab any of them. Burps don't want tickets. They just want to have fun.

But *Louie* wanted those tickets. He was the first one at the Skee-Ball

KA-CHING!

SKEE-
O-
BALL

machine, followed close behind by Max and Mike.

"Grab the tickets!" Louie told his friends. "Grab 'em all."

George's feet ran across the arcade. Alex raced after George. "Dude, we gotta get out of here," he shouted to him.

But the super burp wasn't leaving. It was having too great of a time. So great that it wanted to take a picture—to capture this moment forever. The next

thing George knew, he was sitting on the lap of a girl who was getting her picture taken in the photo booth.

"What are you doing? Get out of here!" the girl shouted.

George wanted to get out. He really did. But he couldn't. George wasn't in charge anymore. The super burp was. And the burp wanted its picture taken.

Flash!

Smooch. The minute the camera snapped, **George's lips planted themselves on the girl's cheek**.

"Ooh, gross," the girl said. "You slobbered all over me."

George agreed. Kissing a girl was gross. And not just because of the slobber. He wanted to say he was sorry. But burps don't apologize. *Ever.*

George jumped off the girl's lap and ran out of the photo booth toward the far end of the arcade.

"He's heading for the ball pit," Julianna told Alex. "He must think there's

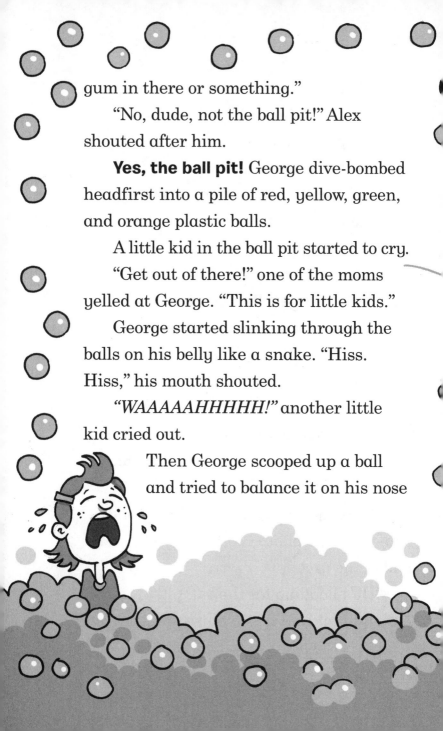

gum in there or something."

"No, dude, not the ball pit!" Alex shouted after him.

Yes, the ball pit! George dive-bombed headfirst into a pile of red, yellow, green, and orange plastic balls.

A little kid in the ball pit started to cry.

"Get out of there!" one of the moms yelled at George. "This is for little kids."

George started slinking through the balls on his belly like a snake. "Hiss. Hiss," his mouth shouted.

"*WAAAAAHHHHH!*" another little kid cried out.

Then George scooped up a ball and tried to balance it on his nose like a seal. His hands started clapping together. His mouth made seal noises. *"Aar, aar, aar."*

Now all the little kids were screaming.

Whoosh! Suddenly, George felt something go pop in the bottom of his belly—like a pin going into a balloon. **All the air rushed out of him.** The super burp was gone. But George was still there—right in the middle of a bunch of crying three-year-olds.

Eww. There was something globby and gooey and covered in toddler spit stuck to George's cheek. He reached up and yanked off a huge piece of freshly chewed gum. *Ouch!* Some of the gum had gotten stuck in his hair. When George pulled the gum off, the hair came with it.

"Don't you think you're a little old to play in the ball pit?" one of the mothers asked him.

George frowned. Sure, *he* thought he was too old to be hanging around with a bunch of little kids in the ball pit. But the super burp hadn't thought so. It thought the ball pit was just right. But how was he supposed to explain that?

George opened his mouth to say, "I'm sorry." And that's exactly what came out.

Then he stood up and climbed out the side of the ball pit—where a security guard was waiting for him.

The guard didn't have to say a word. George knew what he had to do. It was the same thing he always had to do after the burp caused trouble.

Leave.

Chapter 3

"Well, at least you found some gum in the ball pit," Alex told George as they walked into school together the next morning. "That was a good thing."

"Yeah, I guess," George said. But he didn't sound happy. "The super burp's getting worse and worse. **It's showing up everywhere.** At this rate, I'm not going to be allowed in any store, restaurant, or arcade in all of Beaver Brook."

"The security guard didn't say you couldn't come back," Alex pointed out.

"He didn't look like he would be too happy to see me if I did," George said. "Not that I blame him."

"Don't worry. I'll have a cure for you soon," Alex assured George. "I've been checking **The Burp No More Blog** every day. And my mom just got me a subscription to a science magazine called *Gross Stuff Gazette*."

"*Gross Stuff Gazette*?" George repeated. "I've never heard of that one."

"It's new," Alex told him. "It's a magazine about the latest findings on all the gross stuff in the human body. Like boogers, earwax, poop—"

"And *burps*," George said, finishing his sentence.

"Exactly." Alex nodded. "Maybe there will be something about how to stop burps in the first issue."

"I sure hope so," George said. "Because I don't know where or when the burp is going to turn up next."

George walked into the classroom and

sat down at his desk. He looked up at the chalkboard. His teacher, Mrs. Kelly, had written something in big letters:

PICTURE DAY NEXT MONDAY!

George frowned. *I hope it doesn't turn up then*, he thought to himself. *That would be a total disaster.*

"The stuffed dog I won at Quazy Quarters takes up half my room," Julianna told Alex, Chris, and George as they sat down at the lunch table later that day. "My mom said next time I have to get something smaller."

"They have a mini gum-ball machine you can get with one hundred twenty tickets," Alex suggested.

"That gum-ball machine is cool," George agreed. "How come you've never won one of those?"

"I had enough tickets, but **my mom only lets me chew sugarless**," Alex said. "Do you know how hard it is to find sugarless gum balls?"

Just then, Louie, Max, and Mike sat down across the table from George and his buddies.

"Do you want to come over to my

house after school today?" Max asked Louie.

"Hey, I was going to ask him that," Mike told Max.

"**Too bad.** I asked him first," Max told Mike. "So I win."

"He *wins*?" George whispered to Chris, who was sitting next to him. "If Louie's the prize, I'd rather lose."

Chris laughed so hard, he swallowed wrong. **Milk squirted out of his nose.**

"Stop arguing, you guys," Louie told Max and Mike. "I'm not hanging out with *either* of you after school."

Max and Mike stared at Louie. They looked scared.

"You're hanging out with *someone else*?" Max asked nervously.

"You can't," Mike said. "You *always* hang out with us."

"I'm not hanging out with anyone," Louie told them. "I'm spending the afternoon **picking out my outfit for picture day**."

"But picture day is a week away," Mike said.

"I don't even know which of my T-shirts will be clean a week from now," Max added.

"What's the big deal about picture day, anyway?" Mike asked Louie.

George was thinking the exact same

thing as Mike. But George didn't say anything. He didn't want Louie to know he was listening to his conversation. That would make Louie think George was interested in what Louie and his friends were saying. Which he was not. Well, not *really*, anyway.

Louie looked at Mike with surprise. "You're kidding, right?" he asked. "Picture day is a huge deal. It's the day when history is made!"

Now George couldn't even *pretend* not to be paying attention to Louie's conversation. He had to hear this one. **"How is picture day making history?"** he asked Louie.

Louie gave George a snobby smile. "Well, it's probably not for you," Louie told him. "But the picture *I* take next week will wind up in the history books."

Everyone stared at him.

"What are you talking about?" Julianna asked.

"When I'm **rich and famous**, people are going to write books about me," Louie explained. "And they're going to want to put pictures of my life in the books, so my millions of fans can see what I looked like as a kid."

George laughed so hard, he snorted.

"Good one, Louie," he said.

Louie glared at him.

"Oh," George said suddenly. "You were serious. I thought you were making a joke."

"Why would I joke about being rich and famous?" Louie said. "*Of course* that's what I'm going to be when I grow up. Think about it. I'm just a kid and I'm already rich and famous."

"You *totally* are," Mike agreed. He stopped for a minute and thought. "But how?"

"I'm famous because I star in my own webcast, *Life with Louie*," Louie pointed out. "And as for being rich—well, you guys have seen my house."

George thought about pointing out that the house belonged to his parents and no one but a few fourth-graders at Edith B. Sugarman Elementary School ever watched *Life with Louie* webcasts, but he didn't. It would only get him into an argument with Louie. And the new, improved George didn't get into arguments when he could help it.

"I think Louie's right," Sage piped up, suddenly joining the conversation. "It is important to look good in pictures." She turned to George. "Do you think my pink dress would look nice in the class picture, *Georgie*?"

George rolled his eyes. He'd barely noticed that Sage was sitting at the table. But then again, George spent a lot of time trying not to notice Sage. He really hated when she called him *Georgie* and batted her eyelashes up and down at him. It was **just plain creepy**.

Still, Sage wasn't totally wrong. And neither was Louie. A picture *was* forever. And years from now, George hoped his classmates would remember him as a . . .

well . . . um . . . actually, George wasn't
sure what he wanted to be remembered as.
He just knew it was going to be something
a whole lot cooler than being Louie Farley.

Rrrriinnnggg!

That night, while George was doing his
homework, the phone rang. He jumped up
and ran into the hall to get the call.

"Hello?" he said.

"Dude! You're not going to believe this!"
Alex exclaimed.

George laughed. Alex was so excited,
he forgot to say hello.

"What happened?" George asked.

"I measured my ABC gum ball this
afternoon, and it is even bigger than I
had thought. It's bigger
than any ABC gum
ball *ever*!" Alex was
talking so fast, the

words sounded all strung together.

But George understood what Alex was saying. *And* what it meant. **"You broke the record!"** George shouted excitedly. "You have to let the people at the *Schminess Book of World Records* know!"

"I already sent them an e-mail, and they wrote back!" Alex said excitedly. "And the best news is that they're sending this guy named Harris Faris to my house after school on Thursday. He's going to do the **official *Schminess* measurement.**"

"Wow!" George exclaimed. "So you're going to be the world-record holder."

"I hope so. If I measured right," Alex said. "Anyway, since you've helped me make this gum ball possible, do you want to come over on Thursday and wait for the *Schminess* guy with me?"

"Definitely," George assured his best friend. "I'll even chew one more piece before I get there. We'll stick it on for good luck!"

George was really happy for Alex. But as he hung up the phone, he also started to feel kind of rotten. Alex was *really* making history. Not just imagining it, the way Louie was. Alex was going to be remembered for something really, really cool.

But George hadn't done anything cool. He hadn't done anything he would be remembered for.

George shook his head. *Snap out of it,* he told himself. *You're getting as jealous as Louie.*

Gulp. Thinking he was anything like Louie Farley was the most **rotten thought ever**. World-record rotten. George promised himself right then and there that he was never going to be jealous again—at least not if he could help it.

Which was a lot easier said than done.

Chapter 4

"Nice varsity jacket," Chris said to George on the school playground the next morning. "Whose is it?"

"It's mine," George said proudly.

Alex gave him a funny look. *"Yours?"* he asked. "Isn't it a little big?"

Actually, the jacket wasn't a little big—it was *huge*. The sleeves hung down to George's knees. It looked more like a varsity *dress* than a varsity jacket.

"I didn't know you played **varsity football** for the Ripdale Rockets," Chris said. "I didn't even know you ever lived in Ripdale."

George frowned. "Well, I didn't

actually live there. Or play football. My dad did. But he gave me the jacket. So it's mine. I think it makes me look like a **real jock**."

"It does," Chris agreed. "I wish my dad had a varsity jacket he could give me to wear. But he wasn't on any sports teams in high school. He was in the school plays."

"My dad was on the chess team," Alex said. "You don't get a varsity jacket for that, either."

"You guys don't need jackets," George told his friends. He looked at Chris. "Everyone knows you're the fourth-grade artist."

"That's true," Chris agreed.

"And, Alex, you're the school's science whiz," George continued. "No one will ever forget that. But I'm not the fourth-grade anything—at least I wasn't until today.

But now I'm the school jock, like my dad was. That's why I need a varsity jacket. I'm going to wear this jacket every day from now on."

"I never thought of you as a jock," Alex said slowly.

"I'm **the catcher on the fourth-grade baseball team**," George reminded him.

"Maybe you should wear your baseball uniform for the class picture," Chris suggested.

"Nah. A varsity jacket is way cooler," he told Chris. "And jocks are always way cool."

"George, please come to the board and show us how to solve this long-division problem," Mrs. Kelly said when the kids were all seated in the classroom later that morning.

George got up and walked to the

board. He didn't feel all that cool anymore. In fact, he was really hot under the varsity jacket. **A big glob of sweat** was building up on his forehead. His armpits were starting to stink. But there was no way George was taking off his jacket. Jocks wore their varsity jackets everywhere.

George picked up the chalk and started to write on the board.

$23\overline{)592}$

"Five hundred ninety-two divided by twenty-three," George said out loud as he began to write on the board. "Okay. First, you have to figure out how many times twenty-three goes into . . ."

Whoops. The chalk slipped through

his **slippery, sweaty fingers** and landed on the floor. "Sorry," George said as he bent down to pick up the chalk.

Bam! George banged his head on the board as he stood up.

Louie started laughing. "Good thing there's nothing in his head," he joked.

Mike and Max both laughed, too. But they stopped when Mrs. Kelly shot them a look.

"Are you okay?" Mrs. Kelly asked George.

"Sure," George answered. He stood with his back to the board and flashed his teacher a smile. "I'm tough." He flexed his muscles and turned to finish the math problem.

But it was gone.

"Hey, where'd the problem go?"
George asked.

Now *everyone* was laughing.

"Check the back of your jacket," Louie
said. He was laughing the hardest.

George turned his head around as
far as it would go and looked down. Sure
enough, there was chalk all over the back
of his dad's varsity jacket. He'd erased
the whole thing when he'd turned to show

Mrs. Kelly how tough he was.

"George, why don't you sit down?" Mrs. Kelly said. "I'll write another problem on the board and give someone else a try. How about you, Louie?"

Louie smiled smugly as he walked up to the board. "I'll show you how it's done," he told George.

George frowned. He knew how long division was done. He was great at long division. But he wasn't going to be able to prove that today.

Man, being a jock was tougher than it looked.

"You want to play a game of **killer ball**?" Louie asked George that afternoon at recess. He stared at George's dad's varsity jacket. "Come on, Mr. Jock. Show us what you got."

Normally, George would find

something else to do rather than play killer ball. It was a game Louie had made up that was sort of like dodgeball, only meaner. George hated it.

But Louie had made today's game sound like a dare. And if George said no to a dare, **Louie would never let him hear the end of it**.

"Sure, I guess," George said warily. He looked over at Chris and Alex. They nodded. *Phew.* At least George would have his friends on his team.

"You, Alex, and Chris are on one team," Louie said. "Max, Mike, and I are on the other. Get ready for a game of ultimate killer ball!"

George's team lined up on one side of the field. Louie's team lined up on the other. Louie held up the red rubber ball. "We throw first," he said. With that, Louie let the ball fly, hard—right at George.

George tried to run to the side, but his feet got all tangled in the extra-large varsity football jacket. *Wham!* George tripped and fell to the ground.

Alex scooped up a ball and threw it at Mike.

Mike caught the ball in midair and passed it off to Louie. Louie sent the ball soaring again.

TRIP!

George started to untangle his feet and stand up. But before he could—*slam!* George felt the ball bash him right in the stomach.

"You're out!" Louie laughed.

Whoosh! Suddenly George felt all the air rush out of him, like a balloon popping in his belly. It felt a lot like the end of a super burp. Except George hadn't burped.

He was just out. And the only thing that had popped was his dream of being the famous fourth-grade jock.

Chapter 5

"Nice shades, dude," Alex said as he, Chris, and George met up in the school yard before school on Wednesday.

George lowered his sunglasses onto the bridge of his nose and grinned. "Thanks," he said.

"How come you're wearing sunglasses when it's cloudy?" Chris asked.

"I'm wearing them because they're cool," George explained. **"Rock-star cool."**

"You do kind of look like a rock star," Chris agreed.

"Thanks," George replied. "I'm thinking maybe I'll wear these on picture day. Then if I become a rock star when I grow up, people can look back at our class picture and see that I was *always* cool."

"You want to be a musician?" Alex asked. "I didn't know that."

"I'm *already* a musician," George said. "I played the keyboard with **the Runny Noses** at the talent show, remember?"

Alex and Chris both laughed.

"How could I forget?" Alex asked.

"How could *anyone* forget?" Chris added.

George turned red. He knew what his friends were talking about. The super burp had shown up right in the middle of the school talent show. And it had made George dive-bomb off the stage into the audience. George had landed headfirst— *in Principal McKeon's lap*!

"Let's not talk about the talent show," George said. "That's old news, anyway."

"Yeah," Chris agreed. "Besides, we've

got *new* news. Alex, when you get your picture in the *Schminess Book of World Records,* it will be **the biggest thing** in the history of our school since Mrs. Kelly was on that TV show, *Dance Your Pants Off!*"

Wow. Chris was acting like Alex was already famous, and he wasn't even in the book yet. George frowned—for a minute. But then he stopped and tried to force a smile on his face. If he didn't stop getting so jealous, he was going to go down in history for breaking a record, too—the record for world's worst best friend.

Julianna and Sage were standing nearby. Their heads turned when Chris mentioned the *Schminess Book of World Records*.

"Did I hear you say Alex broke the world record for the world's biggest ABC gum ball?" Julianna asked Chris excitedly.

"Uh-huh," Chris told the girls. "A *Schminess* guy is coming to Alex's house to take **the official measurement** tomorrow."

"How come you didn't tell the whole class about it when you found out?" Julianna asked Alex.

"I only told these two guys," Alex explained, looking over at George and Chris. "I kind of didn't want a whole lot of people to know, just in case things don't work out."

"I'm sorry," Chris said. "I didn't realize I was talking so loudly."

"It's okay," Alex assured him. "It was

going to come out sooner or later."

"Can I come to the measuring?" Julianna asked. "I'll videotape the whole thing for my morning announcements sports broadcast. It'll be **a school-news exclusive!**"

"Sure," Alex told her.

"Are you going to be there, Georgie?" Sage asked. She blinked her eyelashes up and down.

George nodded.

"Then I'll come, too," Sage told him. "And maybe I'll wear sunglasses. Yours are so *cute*."

George groaned. Rock stars weren't supposed to be cute. They were supposed to be *cool*. **Didn't Sage know anything?**

Just then, the bell rang. It was time to go inside.

"Let's go, rock star," Alex said to George.

"Right behind you, record breaker," George said to Alex.

George and Alex walked past Louie, Max, and Mike as they headed into the school. Louie hadn't said a word about Alex breaking the record, but George was pretty sure he'd heard all about it. After all, **his humongous left** ear was pointing right toward where Alex had been standing. With ears as big as his, Louie had probably heard every single word.

"Alex isn't the only one breaking a record," Louie announced suddenly as the kids walked into the school building.

He handed Max his cell phone. "Here," Louie said. "I want you to videotape me breaking the record for **the longest time spent skating backward**."

George laughed. *Yep.* Louie had heard the other kids talking. And now he wanted in on the action.

Mike looked at Louie and frowned. "How come *Max* gets to tape you skating?" he asked. "I want to help you break a record, too."

"You can be the one who tells me when to turn, so I don't bump into stuff when I'm going backward," Louie told him. Then he popped the wheels out from the bottoms of his sneakers and started roller-skating backward down the hallway.

"Turn to your left," Mike told Louie.

Louie turned and kept on skating. "We'll show this on *Life with Louie* tonight," he said. "It will get us record-breaking ratings."

"Turn right," Mike told Louie.

But Louie was **too busy talking to listen** to Mike. "I wonder if a guy can get two pages in the *Schminess Book of World Records*."

"Louie, TURN RIGHT," Mike repeated louder. "Louie . . ."

Slam! Louie skated right into Principal McKeon!

"LOUIE FARLEY!" the principal exclaimed. "What are you doing?"

The kids in the hall all stopped and turned to see what was happening.

"I was breaking a world record," Louie tried to explain.

"For being unsafe in the school hallway?" Principal McKeon asked.

"No, for roller-skating backward," Louie corrected her.

Principal McKeon shook her head. "You know you're not supposed to have a cell phone in school," she told Max.

"It's Louie's," Max explained nervously.

Louie glared at him.

"Hand it over now," the principal told Max. She turned to Louie. "I'll give it back to you after school when we call your parents. Now pop those wheels back into your shoes, and go to class the correct way."

George grinned. It was nice seeing someone *else* get into trouble for a change. Especially when that someone was Louie Farley.

"The science quiz was really hard," George complained later that afternoon as he and Alex stood in line for lunch. "I think I got half the questions wrong."

"You should have taken your sunglasses off," Alex told him. "The questions

are easier to answer when you can see them."

"That's true," George said. "But rock stars **never** take off their sunglasses."

George put his tray down on the metal shelf and reached for his food. He grabbed **a hot dog and a bowl of vanilla ice cream**.

"Um, dude," Alex said. "I thought you hated . . ."

George didn't hear the rest of what Alex said. He'd already started carrying his tray toward the lunch table.

He sat down and looked at his lunch. Behind the dark glasses, George could barely see a thing. But he knew he was going to eat his lunch the way he liked best. **Backward!** That meant dessert first. George picked up his spoon and dug into the bowl of vanilla ice cream.

Except it *wasn't* vanilla ice cream. It was **creamy clam chowder**. *Yuck!* George hated clam chowder. The clams were all chewy—they tasted like pieces of rubber dipped in hot milk. He made a face and spit a clam into his napkin.

"I tried to warn you, dude," Alex said.

"It looked like ice cream from behind my sunglasses," George said with a sigh. "All I saw was something creamy in a bowl." He looked down at his tray. "That's really a hot dog, though, right?"

"Yeah," Alex told him. "You can eat that."

George frowned as he took a bite of his hot dog. In the past two days, he'd whacked his head on the blackboard, taken a flying killer ball to the gut, bombed his science test, and chewed a rubbery, milky clam—and the super burp had made him kiss a girl. *Blech.*

This going-down-in-history thing was a whole lot tougher than he'd ever imagined.

Chapter 6

"Yo, dudes!" Alex exclaimed as George and Chris walked into the shed behind Alex's house on Thursday afternoon after school. "You made it."

"I told you I'd be here," George said. "No way would I ever miss this. I just had to run by home real quick to change." He took off his cowboy hat because it was blocking his view of the ABC gum ball. **"That's amazing!"** he exclaimed.

"Huge," Chris added.

"I hope it's huge enough," Alex said. "I measured it three more times this afternoon, just to be sure."

"Look what I made for you," Chris

said. He held up a poster that read:

The letters were formed with gum balls that had been glued to the paper.

"No congratulations yet," Alex told him. "Not until Harris Faris gets here to measure it and say I *officially* broke the record."

Just then, Julianna and Sage walked into the shed. Sage hurried over to stand by George. George hurried across the room to stand away from Sage.

"Has the *Schminess* guy gotten here yet?" Julianna asked.

"Nope," Alex told her. "Any minute, I think."

"Good," Julianna said. She took her video camera out of the case. "I want to get every second of this on tape."

"Georgie, I love your cowboy hat," Sage said. "I have one just like it at home. Except it's purple."

George rolled his eyes. A purple cowboy hat wasn't a genuine cowboy hat. Cowboys usually wore brown or black hats. George knew because he had seen real cowboys during a trip his family had taken to a dude ranch.

But George didn't have time to argue with Sage now. Other kids were already arriving to see the official measuring. Most were fourth-graders. But there were some fifth-graders, too. Word had definitely spread.

Alex's mom followed the group of kids

into the shed. She was carrying a big shopping bag. "Hi, kids," she greeted them. "I've got something special to give each one of you as a souvenir for Alex's big day."

"Mom . . . you shouldn't have," Alex told her. But he was smiling.

Alex's mom started pulling **toothbrushes and dental floss** out of her bag. "After you chew, remember to brush and floss," she reminded the kids. "Here, let me show you."

Alex's mom shoved a strand of floss between her teeth and pulled it back and forth. Then she held it up for everyone to see. **A chunk of green gunk was stuck to the floss.**

"Look at that big piece of broccoli," she

said. "If I hadn't flossed, that could have been stuck between my teeth for weeks. Or until I swallowed it. And broccoli doesn't taste better the second time around, believe me."

Alex's smile drooped. "Mom," he groaned. "You REALLY shouldn't have."

George felt Alex's pain. **Moms could be embarrassing sometimes.** This was *definitely* one of those times.

George shoved a piece of green gum into his mouth. Maybe he had time to add one more piece to Alex's gum ball before Harris Faris arrived.

"You guys, I think he's here!" Chris shouted excitedly from the back of the shed. "I heard a car pull up out front."

"Whoa," Alex said.

George glanced over at his buddy. He looked nervous.

Unfortunately, Alex wasn't the only one who was scared. George was afraid, too. He was afraid of what was brewing in his belly. There was something bubbly and bouncy down there. And it was going wild.

The super burp was back!

Oh no. George couldn't let the burp escape. Not at **the most important moment** in his best friend's life. He had to squelch the belch.

George shut his lips tight to keep the burp from escaping. But the burp was strong. *Bing-bong. Ping-pong.* The bubbles were kickboxing his kidneys and spinning on his spleen.

Ping-pong. Bing-bong. The bubbles cling-clanged through his colon and hip-hopped up to his heart. George swallowed hard, trying to push the burp back down. But the burp fought back. Bubbles tap-danced on his tongue and twirled around his teeth. *Tap, tap. Twirl, twirl . . .*

The kids in the shed all turned and stared at George.

"Dude, no!" Alex shouted.

Dude, *yes. Right here. Right now.* The burp was out. And it wanted to play! The next thing George knew, his finger had shoved itself into his mouth. It was grabbing his gum and pulling it out in a long, skinny string.

"George, please put that gum back in your mouth," Alex's mom insisted.

George wanted to put the gum back in his mouth. He really did. But the burp had something more fun in mind. So

George's finger kept pulling. Longer . . .
longer . . . longer. Soon George had **a
slippery, slimy rope of gooey green gum**
hanging from his mouth.

"Yeehaw!" George swung the gooey,
gummy rope around his head like a lasso.
"Yeehaw!"

Ooey-gooey gum spit flew all around
and rained down on the kids in the shed.

"Watch it!" Julianna yelled at him.
"You're getting spit on my camera lens."

Sage hid under the tool bench. "Not in
my hair, Georgie," she said.

"Yippie-ki-yay!" George shouted
loudly. He twirled the green
gum lasso faster and faster.
"Waaaahhhooooo!"

"George, chewing gum is not a toy!" Alex's mom scolded.

Maybe not, but the super burp sure was having fun playing with it. George twirled the gum harder. More **ooey-gooey gum spit** flew across the room.

George put his gum back in his mouth. He raced over to the ABC gum ball and broke off a massive chunk.

"Dude! Don't!" Alex shouted. "I need every single piece if I'm going to break the record."

"**You're ruining everything**," Alex's mom told George. "What kind of friend are you?"

George was a really good friend. But the burp wasn't. It was a selfish, terrible, doesn't-care-about-anyone-else kind of friend. And it was in charge now. So George started to shove the chunk of ABC gum into his mouth.

"George, **don't you dare** put that in your mouth," Alex's mom shouted. "You don't know where it's been."

"Sure, I do," George's mouth replied. "It's been on Alex's gum ball."

"Put that big chunk of gum back!" Alex shouted. "Please, dude!"

But the burp had no intention of putting that hunk of gum back. George's hand started heading for his mouth and . . .

Whoosh! George felt all the air rush out of him. The super burp was gone. But George was still there, with the big chunk of ABC gum in his hands.

Quickly, George walked over to Alex's giant ABC gum ball and shoved the gum back on the ball. Then he pulled the piece he had been chewing out of his mouth and planted it on top. "One last piece," he told his best friend. "For luck."

"Uh . . . thanks," Alex mumbled.

"Young man, that was **quite a burp**!" a man's voice bellowed suddenly.

George turned to see a short guy in a *Schminess Book of World Records* blazer walking toward him.

"Do you *always* burp like that?" Harris Faris asked George.

"Well . . . I . . . ," George began.

"Sometimes he burps even louder," Chris interrupted.

"Impressive," Mr. Faris said. "That might be **a record-breaking burp**. If you're ever interested in finding out, you should stop by my office. We can measure the sound level to see if it qualifies as the world's loudest burp."

"You can do that?" George asked.

"Sure," he replied. "All you have to do is burp into our SPL meter."

"A what?" George asked.

"SPL meter," Alex chimed in. "It stands for 'sound pressure level.' It's a machine that measures decibels—how loud something is. I read about it in one of my science books."

"I don't know if the burp will pop out while I'm sitting in front of a machine," George explained. "It just sort of comes up when it wants to." But he took Mr. Faris's card, anyway.

"Wait just a minute!" Suddenly Louie's voice rang out from the path leading up to the shed. "I'll take your card," he shouted.

Louie started to run across the lawn toward the shed. George looked at him curiously. Louie seemed to have gained fifty pounds since school let out. He was *huge*.

"Hurry up," Louie called to Mike and Max, who were following right behind him—as usual. "And keep that camera on. We have to capture every minute of this."

The path was icy. Louie ran a few more steps and then . . . *SPLAT!* He fell **flat on his face**. George sure hoped Mike and Max had captured *that*!

Louie tried to stand. But he couldn't. His legs wouldn't bend.

"What's wrong with you?" George asked Louie.

"Nothing," Louie answered. "It's just hard to get up when you're wearing *twenty-seven pairs of snow pants*." He looked up at Harris Faris. "That's the world record, right?"

"Wrong," Mr. Faris answered. "That was last year's record. A few weeks ago a guy in Tajikistan put on **twenty-nine** pairs of snow pants. He's the new record holder."

Louie looked like he'd been punched in the gut. Or like he wanted to punch someone *else* in the gut. Either way, he was really mad—and hot.

Harris Faris pulled his official measuring tape out of his pocket and walked over to the gum ball. "Okay, let's measure this thing," he said.

George's heart started pounding so

hard it felt as though it could pound its way right out of his chest and go bouncing across the floor. **"This is it,"** he whispered to Alex. "Good luck."

Chapter 7

Harris Faris carefully wrapped the official *Schminess Book of World Records* measuring tape around the gum ball. He pulled it tight—but not so tight that it would squish any gum that hadn't completely hardened. Then he held the measuring tape with his thumb and looked at the numbers.

George rolled his eyes. How long could it possibly take to read a number on a measuring tape?

Harris Faris pulled out a small camera and snapped a picture of the numbers on the measuring tape.

Come on, George thought to himself.

Say something already.

Finally, Mr. Faris looked out at the crowd of kids. "The circumference of this gum ball is **one thousand, six hundred twenty-five millimeters and four micrometers**," he announced.

Is that big enough?

George looked nervously at Alex.

Uh-oh. Alex wasn't smiling. But then again, he wasn't frowning. Or moving. He was frozen in place.

George couldn't wait any longer. "What does that mean?" he asked.

"It means that Alex is officially the world-record holder for the largest ABC gum ball built by someone under the age of eighteen!" Harris Faris replied.

A big grin broke out across Alex's face.

George smiled, too. But not so big. That old jealousy thing was nagging at him again. Alex really was going down in history. It was something no other kid at Edith B. Sugarman Elementary School had done before. George wished he had been the one to do that.

Then, out of the corner of his eye, George spotted Louie. His face was all red and angry. His eyes were scrunched up into jealous little slits.

The last thing George wanted was to be like *that*. So George forced an even bigger smile onto his face and pumped his fist in the air. **"Alex! Alex! Alex!"** he cheered.

Chris and Sage joined in. "Alex! Alex! Alex!"

Before long, everyone was cheering for Alex. Well, everyone except Louie, anyway. He was too busy trying to stand up. Besides, Louie only cheered for Louie.

Harris Faris grinned at Alex. "Young man, you have just become a junior world-record holder. And that means you're going to San Luis Obispo!"

Huh? The kids stopped cheering and stared at him.

"He's going *where*?" George asked.

"San Luis Obispo, California," Mr. Faris repeated.

"I know where that is!" Alex said excitedly. "San Luis Obispo, California, is home to **the world-famous Bubble Gum Alley**. The walls in the alley are covered in ABC gum that's been stuck on by tourists from all over the world. I saw it in a book I read about the history of chewing gum."

"Exactly," Mr. Faris said. "It's the perfect backdrop for your official *Schminess Book of World Records* photograph."

"Wow! I'm going to California!" Alex exclaimed.

"Yep," Harris Faris told him. "This weekend. You, your family, and the friend of your choice."

"I choose George," Alex said immediately.

"Me?" George asked excitedly. "You want *me* to go with you to Bubble Gum Alley?"

"Sure," Alex told him. "Who else?"

Alex really was a great friend. Now George felt even more guilty about being jealous of him. George knew that Alex had worked really hard to be in the *Schminess Book of World Records*. He *deserved* to be in it. In fact, Alex should be in the book twice—once for the world's largest ABC gum ball and once for being the world's greatest best friend.

"Wow! First class," George said as he took his seat across the aisle from Alex on the airplane on Saturday morning. "I don't think even my *parents* have flown first class before."

"The *Schminess* people sure know how to do things right," Alex's mom said.

"Make sure the gum ball is belted in for takeoff, son," Alex's dad reminded him.

"It is," Alex assured his dad.

Some of the other people in first class had given Alex strange looks when he'd placed the gum ball on the seat next to him and buckled it in. But George didn't think it was strange at all. *Of course* the gum ball had a first-class seat. It was **the guest of honor**, after all.

"Here you go, boys," Alex's mom said. "Chew this gum when we take off. It will keep your ears from popping."

George looked at her strangely. "*You're* telling us to chew gum?"

"It's sugarless," Alex's mom told him. Then she gave George a stern look. "Just make sure you keep it in your mouth."

George frowned. He wished the stupid super burp hadn't gotten him into trouble with his best friend's mom. He wanted to tell her it wasn't his fault. It was the burp's fault. But George knew she wouldn't believe him, even if he did. So instead, he just said, "Yes, ma'am."

George sat back in his seat and chewed his gum as the plane raced down the runway. He listened carefully as the flight attendant told them about emergency exits and oxygen masks. He kept his seat belt buckled and his seat in the upright position for takeoff. George was **determined not to cause anyone any trouble.**

Once they were in the air, George reached into his backpack and pulled out his copy of last year's *Schminess Book of World Records*. He'd bought it at the book fair at his old school in Cherrydale, way before he'd even moved to Beaver Brook. Back then, George never dreamed that his new best friend was going to be in the *Schminess Book of World Records*—or that he'd be flying all the way to California to see him photographed for it.

There was something else George could never have imagined back when he lived in Cherrydale. And that was something that bing-bonged and ping-ponged. Something that was brewing—*right now*—in the bottom of his belly.

Oh no! Not the super burp. **Not at 30,000 feet in the air!**

Oh yes! The magical super burp had followed George way up into the sky.

And now it was ready for **some in-flight entertainment**. An ABC gum ball might be happy being strapped down in a seat— but a super burp was not. No way was it being kept down.

The burp was ready for takeoff. It bounced out of his belly, lunged at his liver, crashed into his colon, edged up his esophagus, and . . .

George let out a super burp so loud, you could probably hear it 30,000 feet away—back down on the ground.

"Uh-oh . . ." Alex gulped.

"George!" Alex's mom scolded. "What do you say?"

George opened his mouth to say,

"Excuse me." But that's not what came out. Instead, George shouted, "Coffee? Tea? How about ME?!"

George's hands unhooked his seat belt. His legs bolted out into the aisle and ran to where a flight attendant was wheeling out a snack cart.

"Look out! Here comes a goofy foot!" George leaped on top of the snack cart and started **skateboarding down the aisle**.

"Young man! I'll have to ask you to go back to your seat!" the flight attendant shouted.

George wanted to go back to his seat. He really did. But the burp was tired of sitting. It wanted to have fun! And fun meant skateboarding down the aisle on the snack cart. He moved his right foot back and his left foot forward. "Switch stance."

"Who does this boy belong to?" the flight attendant demanded.

Alex's mom was in such shock, she couldn't even open her mouth.

"Cookies? Pretzels?" George asked the passengers. He started throwing teeny packets of snacks at the people in the seats. He reached down and grabbed a can of soda. Then his hands started shaking it up and down.

"Oh no you don't!" the flight attendant shouted. She snatched the can from George's hands. She tried to pull him down off the cart.

But the burp had made George fast and strong. Quickly, he opened an overhead bin, pulled himself up, and curled up inside.

"Get down from there!" the flight attendant yelled.

Whoosh! Just then, George felt something go pop in the bottom of his belly. The super burp was gone.

But George was still curled up inside an overhead bin on an airplane flying 30,000 feet in the air. He opened his mouth to say, "I'm sorry." And that's exactly what came out.

"Get down," the flight attendant repeated.

"Yes, ma'am," George said quietly. He climbed out of the bin and dropped to the floor—being careful not to step on the woman sitting in the seat below.

"Now go back to your seat," the flight attendant told George. **And do not get up for the rest of this flight."**

"But what if I have to go to the bathroom?" George asked her.

"Hold it in!" the flight attendant told him.

George frowned. He wasn't very good at holding things in. Hadn't he just proved that?

Chapter 8

"Wow!" Alex exclaimed. "I feel like I've arrived in **ABC gum heaven**!"

George grinned. He could see why Alex might feel that way. Bubble Gum Alley was a long narrow street with gum stuck to the walls on either side. There were thousands and thousands of pieces— blue gum, red gum, purple gum, green gum, and even black gum. Some pieces were stringy; others were thick globs. Some still had pieces of the wrappers stuck to them. George had never seen so much ABC gum in his whole life— not even on Alex's gum ball.

"Okay, Alex, let's get a picture of you and your record-breaking gum ball right here with the wall of gum behind you," the *Schminess* photographer said.

George stood behind the photographer, next to Alex's parents. He watched as the photographer's assistant placed Alex's gum ball on a wooden platform and adjusted the lighting so Alex and the gum ball would both look good in the picture. It seemed to take a very long time.

Finally the photographer got ready to take the picture. Alex stood proudly next to his gigantic ABC gum ball and got ready to say cheese.

And that's when George felt it—that
rumbling feeling at the bottom of his
belly. *Bing-bong. Ping-pong.* OH NO! The
super burp was back.

This was *ba-a-ad*! George couldn't let
the burp ruin Alex's big moment. He just
had to **squelch this belch**!

George quickly spun into action. And
boy did he spin! George twirled around
and around, trying to force the burp down
into his toes, like water spinning its way
down a drain.

"George!" Alex's mother yelled. "Stop
that this instant!"

But George *couldn't* stop. *Bing-bong.
Ping-pong! Ding-dong!* The bubbles were
bouncing all around, trying to force their
way up and out.

"Dude, not again!" Alex yelled. "Not
here. Not now."

George shook his head. No. *Not* here.

Not now. There was no way George was going to let the super burp ruin Alex's *Schminess Book of World Records* photo shoot. No matter how jealous he had been of Alex, there was no way he was going to let anything ruin this day. Not even the magical super burp. George spun faster, trying to force that burp back down.

Whirr, whirr, whirr. George was spinning so hard, he was getting dizzy. His eyes seemed to be rolling around in his head. He couldn't even see where he was going. He spun around the alley, past Alex. Past the ABC gum ball. Past . . .

Splat! George **slammed right into the wall** of Bubble Gum Alley.

Whoosh! George felt all the air rush right out of him. It was as if someone had taken a pin and popped a giant balloon in the bottom of his belly.

George raised his fist in the air! In the battle of boy versus burp, George had emerged victorious! The belch had been squelched!

The burp might have disappeared, but George was still there—stuck to the wall of Bubble Gum Alley. He'd spun his way right into some huge, sticky globs of freshly chewed ABC gum. They were holding him there like glue. But George didn't mind. He couldn't get into any trouble if he was stuck to a wall. **For once, that stupid super burp had done him a favor.**

"Hey, that's pretty funny," the photographer said. "Kid, stay right there in the background by the wall. Don't move."

"No problem," George said. Which it wasn't. Because George *couldn't* move. He was stuck.

"Okay, Alex. Smile and say, 'Gum ball'!" the photographer said.

Alex grinned. **"GUM BALL!"** he shouted.

Chapter 9

"So the whole alley is covered in ABC gum?" Chris asked as he and some of the other fourth-graders gathered on the playground on Monday morning. They were all looking at the photos Alex and George had brought back from California.

"Just the walls," George told him. "If there was gum on the ground, it would get stuck to your shoes."

"They've got **ABC gum from all over the world** stuck to the walls of Bubble Gum Alley," Alex said. "People who are really into gum travel to San Luis Obispo, just to make sure their country is represented."

"Do you have a copy of the actual photo that they're going to use in the *Schminess Book of World Records*?" Julianna asked Alex.

Alex nodded and pulled out a photo. It showed him smiling broadly and standing next to the giant ABC gum ball. George was in the background, stuck to the wall. His face was a little out of focus, and he looked tiny compared to Alex, but you could definitely tell it was George.

Millions of kids all over the world were going to see that picture. They would know George was there when the *Schminess Book of World Records* photographed the junior world-record holder for the largest ABC gum ball. And he had been there because he was Alex's best friend. So George was kind of going down in history, too—for being a good friend.

He hadn't even needed to wear a big sweaty jacket or dark sunglasses to do it. **He just needed to be himself.**

"Perfect," Julianna said. "I'll show the picture on morning announcements."

Just then, Louie walked onto the playground, trailed by Mike and Max. George looked over to see what Louie was wearing. After all, it was picture day, and Louie had made such a big deal about dressing for the history books.

George was really surprised by Louie's outfit. Mostly because Louie looked exactly like . . . well . . . Louie. He was wearing his usual T-shirt, jeans, and sneakers. He hadn't even gotten a haircut.

"What happened to dressing to show everyone how rich and ready for fame you were in fourth grade?" George asked him.

"My mom didn't have time to take me

shopping," Louie said with a frown. "She said I could borrow some stuff from my older brother, Sam, if I wanted to wear something different. But I didn't want to go down in history wearing someone else's clothes."

Louie might not have dressed for picture day, but George had. He was wearing **his skateboarding clothes**—a belt with the skateboard buckle, loose-fitting black jeans, and a T-shirt with a skateboarder on it that said KING OF THE SIDEWALK. He'd even spiked his hair with gel—to make himself look extra cool. He was **George Brown, Skater Dude!**

"Okay. George, Alex, Louie, and

Mike, go up on the top stair of the stage," Mrs. Kelly said later that morning as the class lined up for picture day. "You will stand up in the back row while the others sit on chairs in the front row."

As Mrs. Kelly arranged the other kids in the class, Alex stood next to George, reading his new *Gross Stuff Gazette*. George shook his head in amazement. Alex sure was taking this class science-guy thing seriously. Whoever heard of someone reading in the middle of getting ready for his class picture?

"Dude, you gotta take off your belt," Alex whispered to George.

"I have to what?" George asked him.

"Take off your belt," Alex said. He pointed to the article he had been reading in the *Gross Stuff Gazette*. "It's right here in the magazine. Belts squeeze the air out of your stomach and make the burps come out."

"But I can't take off my belt," George said. "If I do . . ."

Alex didn't wait for George to finish his sentence. He reached over and unhooked George's belt for him.

"You gotta do it," Alex insisted. "This is the cure. I'm sure of it." **He yanked the belt from George's pants.**

"Say cheese!" the photographer said.

Whoops. At just that minute, George's loose-fitting jeans fell down around his knees.

Louie nearly exploded with laughter. **"Check out George's tighty whities!"**

Mrs. Kelly turned around. "George!" she exclaimed. "Pull your pants up. What were you thinking?"

"I'm sorry," George gasped, pulling his pants back up. "They're just a little bit big."

"That's why you need to wear a belt," Mrs. Kelly reminded him.

George could feel his face turning red as he and put his belt back on. The kids were all laughing now. George looked over at Alex.

"I'm sorry, dude," Alex said.

George could tell he meant it. Besides, George wasn't mad at Alex. He had only been trying to help. But even a smart kid like Alex was no match for the magical super burp. That burp wasn't going away anytime soon. It was going to keep coming back again and again to make George do goofy stuff.

As he stood there buckling his belt, George had a horrible thought: Years from now, when the other kids looked at their fourth-grade class picture, they would all be thinking of him as George Brown, Class Clown—exactly the guy he was trying so hard *not* to be.

Grrr. Stupid super burp. Even when it wasn't around, it still managed to ruin everything.

About the Author

Nancy Krulik is the author of more than 150 books for children and young adults including three *New York Times* Best Sellers and the popular Katie Kazoo, Switcheroo books. She lives in New York City with her family, and many of George Brown's escapades are based on things her own kids have done. (No one delivers a good burp quite like Nancy's son, Ian!) Nancy's favorite thing to do is laugh, which comes in pretty handy when you're trying to write funny books!

About the Illustrator

Aaron Blecha was raised by a school of giant squid in Wisconsin and now lives with his family by the south English seaside. He works as an artist designing funny characters, animating cartoons, and illustrating books—including the one you're holding and the Harry Hammer shark series. You can enjoy more of his weird creations at www.monstersquid.com.